Ballet School

Camilla Jessel

PUFFIN BOOKS

PUFFIN BOOKS

Published by the Penguin Group
Penguin Books Ltd, 27 Wrights Lane, London W8 5TZ, England
Penguin Putnam Inc., 375 Hudson Street, New York, New York 10014, USA
Penguin Books Australia Ltd, Ringwood, Victoria, Australia
Penguin Books Canada Ltd, 10 Alcorn Avenue, Toronto, Ontario, Canada M4V 3B2
Penguin Books (NZ) Ltd, Private Bag 102902, NSMC, Auckland, New Zealand

Penguin Books Ltd, Registered Offices: Harmondsworth, Middlesex, England

On the World Wide Web at: www.penguin.com

First published by Hamish Hamilton 1999
Published in Puffin Books 2000
1 3 5 7 9 10 8 6 4 2

Set in Bembo and Poetica

Printed in Singapore by Imago Publishing Limited

British Library Cataloguing in Publication Data
A CIP catalogue record for this book is available from the British Library

ISBN 0–140–38609–2

Contents

Introduction ∞

A ballet dancer needs many years of training — even more than a football player or other athletes. Boys and girls who enjoy classical ballet often start working quite seriously by the age of eight or nine. To become professional dancers and eventually perfect all the most difficult jumps and turns, they will need to begin intensive daily classes by the time they are eleven.

Children who study ballet seriously usually do well in all subjects. It helps them with sport and with balance generally, and often improves their concentration at school.

Most boys and girls enjoy dancing just for fun, but some yearn to be able to achieve the daring leaps and lifts they have seen in ballets on television or in the theatre. They may be fascinated by dazzling footwork, or want to dance poetically to music. They may long to perform romantic stories in ballets like *Cinderella*, or prefer modern ballets with tragic, mysterious or witty ideas. Perhaps they dream of creating their own work. Ballet is a challenging and exciting art; there is much to learn besides the sheer physical mastery.

Children who choose to dedicate their lives to dance must find the best possible teachers. They also need to know if their body is flexible enough and a suitable shape for training as a classical dancer.

This book takes you inside one of the greatest ballet schools in the world and shows you how some of today's most talented young dancers learn to develop their extraordinary skills. The Royal Ballet School in England provides performers not only for the Royal Ballet Company but for dance companies across the world. The pupils of the school come from many different countries.

First auditions

Auditions for the Royal Ballet Lower School are held each year all over Britain. About a thousand boys and girls take part, most of them ten or eleven years old, but anyone up to the age of fourteen can apply. Children living in other countries can send a video of their dancing: the most promising will be invited to final auditions in March.

No one needs to have passed ballet examinations or to have won prizes in competitions. The eleven-year-old girls should not yet have begun working on *pointe* (starting too young can ruin a girl's feet for ever). Several boys who come for auditions, and even some girls, have never had ballet lessons. If they are talented enough, they will be able to catch up. In the first year at the Royal Ballet School all pupils start from the beginning, to make sure that they learn everything in the pure Royal Ballet style.

For the auditions the children have numbers pinned on them. Then a friendly ballet teacher shows them exactly what to do. It is almost like an ordinary dancing class with piano music. No one is asked to demonstrate advanced ballet steps.

The auditioners are always pleased to see young people who have already worked hard at dance technique and are keen to study further, but even more important is

their potential: how each child might develop as a dancer in the future.

The school is looking for boys and girls who move naturally to music and who have been born with the right sort of physique to train. Professional dancers need neat, supple bodies, fine bones and straight, slim legs. They must show that they can stretch backwards, forwards, sideways and have extra-flexible hip joints so that they can turn their legs outward into correct ballet positions.

They do not have to be able to do the splits (it is dangerous to try too hard if you cannot do this naturally), but they must have excellent balance, strong, flexible feet and enough bounce to jump high into the air.

As well as having the right physique and a deep sensitivity to music, they must be eager to learn, because classical training involves hard work every day.

Final auditions ∞

Only those with a real chance of getting into the school are invited to the final auditions.

The auditioners, all dancers and teachers themselves, sit at a long table and watch each child carefully. They want to find boys and girls who move beautifully and can express feelings through their dancing. They can see who is musical just by watching each child walk across the room to a simple tune on the piano. They can tell as a boy leaps whether he loves to dance and if he is likely to work hard to perfect his skills.

The final auditions last a whole weekend and there is a lot of nervousness about the results. The tests are harder than at the first auditions, with more steps, stretches and jumps in the ballet studio, more balancing and bending, more examinations of feet, more dancing to see who has imagination and artistic talent.

True dancers are born with the gifts of deep musicality, exceptional suppleness and natural ability to control and coordinate their movements. Without these inborn gifts, it is virtually impossible to become a first-class classical dancer. This is why sometimes the auditioners do not select the children who have passed most exams, but choose others who have very special qualities which can turn them into wonderful dancers after training and hard work.

After the long ballet auditions, each child has a medical examination by a bone specialist. They take intelligence tests and meet the academic teachers, because they will have to keep up with their normal school work as well as the demanding dance studies. Together with their parents, they are shown around the school and see the dormitories where they will sleep (unless they happen to live close by).

By the end of the weekend, most of them have made new friends and are anxious to know if they will be chosen to start at the school the following September. The results come by letter a few days later.

Those who are not selected usually keep up ballet as a hobby with teachers near their homes. Some of them work with such dedication that they manage, even without full-time training, to become professional dancers. Some of them may re-audition the next year, or perhaps at fifteen for the Royal Ballet Upper School.

The children who are chosen for the Royal Ballet Lower School understand that right from the beginning they will have to work very hard to succeed in one of the most difficult professions in the world.

So many shoes! ∞

September has come around and it is the first day of term at the Royal Ballet School. There are fourteen new boys and twenty-one new girls. Before any of the pupils can dance a single step, they must have shoes that fit them precisely.

They do not go to the shoe shop; instead, the shoe shop comes to the school. Each boy must have six new pairs of white canvas ballet shoes (two will be kept clean for important occasions; the other four will get worn out in the first term). The girls get five pairs of pink soft-leather shoes and two pairs of *pointe* shoes, ready for when they have worked hard enough to strengthen their feet. Everyone has to learn to sew on their own elastic and name tapes.

The older pupils use even more shoes. The fourth- and fifth-year girls wear through at least eight pairs of *pointe* shoes in the summer term, because there are many public performances and they always must have fresh, firm shoes.

Looking neat

Dancers must always look neat and tidy. Every day they must have clean leotards and tights or socks. Each time they put on their shoes, they must check that the elastic or ribbons are secure. They must always carry spare shoes in case the elastic breaks or the ribbons come undone.

The girls have to learn how to do their hair, and must always keep it smooth and out of the way.

First ballet classes

∞ barre

Most of the new pupils at the school recognize each other from the auditions.

Now in their first ballet class they meet their teacher, who is going to be the most important person in their dancing life for the next year. All the teachers in the school are professional dancers who have worked with the Royal Ballet or other famous ballet companies. Most of them have now retired from the stage and want to share their lifelong knowledge and great experience of classical dance with the pupils of the school.

The pupils wear name tags at first. The teacher has not only to learn their names but also to remember exactly what each of them needs to work on most.

All pupils are different. Some have particular difficulty with their feet, while others have to battle to perfect the posture of their heads and necks, and yet others need to work on the turn-out of their hips. Some are better at balancing, others at jumping. They all have to practise extra hard at what they cannot do.

Of course, all the children selected for the Royal Ballet School have the makings of good dancers, but now they have to start again from the beginning, learning everything more thoroughly. They have to understand from the inside every movement their body makes.

They learn to sense the muscles inside the back of their legs and tighten them till their knees are flat. 'Pull up from your tummy,' the teacher says. 'Get those stomach muscles really strong!' A pulled-in tummy holds a dancer steady, then she can move her head, arms and legs freely, and can bend in all directions.

More and more instructions. On the exact beat of the music, they swing their legs up in a perfect right angle, their feet pointed. At the same time their teacher says, 'Keep your shoulders down and make your neck longer, chin up.' Each finger must be in place and their heads must follow the lines of their arms.

There is so much to think about, so much detail to remember!

First ballet classes
∞ centre

The pupils work at the *barre* for about an hour, then they come into the centre for a good stretch. In the next hour they repeat most of the exercises without the support of the *barre* to help them balance.

Jumping is one of the most exciting parts of ballet training. This comes towards the end of the class, when pupils are well warmed up. Their teacher watches to see that they are getting high enough off the ground and pointing their toes.

When the class is over, the dancers make their *révérences* (bows or curtsies), not just expressing their thanks to their teacher and the pianist but also showing their respect for the art of ballet.

They have to remember carefully what they have learned in class, write notes and practise in their spare time ready for tomorrow's class. This is only their first week. They have years and years of ballet classes ahead of them.

School work & sport ∞

Ballet class lasts for just two hours every school day. After regular school hours, time may be taken up with folk dance, choreography, rehearsals or other dance activities – not least, practise for next day's class. However, pupils are not dancing all the time. Most of the mornings and afternoons are filled with ordinary school work.

It is vital for young dancers to have a good education so that they can find other work when they retire from dancing. The ballet-school children take the same examinations as other children in England and Wales, in just as many subjects and usually with excellent results.

Dancing is a risky profession and most dancers retire by the age of forty; many change profession earlier. If accidents happen or anything else goes wrong, a thorough education means they will be able to step into a variety of careers without difficulty. Whatever dancers take up when they have finished dancing, they tend to do extremely well because

they are used to concentration and hard work in class and on stage, and are highly self-disciplined.

Sport is always popular with the young dancers. They swim, play tennis and football, and are brilliant netball players because they can jump so high. They are better at gym than most schoolchildren and can make all sorts of exciting shapes in the air (which they may find useful later when they are creating their own ballets).

Art & music ❦

The art of ballet is the combination of movement and music. It is not enough to only know the steps and have the technical skills. Dancers must learn to understand classical music. They have to be able to find sadness, happiness, anger or love in the

music and express poetic feelings as they perform. They will become better dancers if they can recognize the patterns of harmonies and interpret complicated rhythms.

Rhythm is crucial for dancers. You can see at once if someone in the line of dancers is not listening or counting the beats – her leg arrives at the top of the movement before or after everyone else's.

Most of the pupils study one or two musical instruments and they all participate in choral concerts. This is an essential part of their training.

❦

Dancers also need to enjoy and understand visual art. They will work with costume designers and stage designers, and will have to become skilled at putting on their own make-up. The ballet-school children are encouraged to enjoy drawing and painting, and sometimes they make masks.

Acting is important as well. They often put on plays or act out the stories they have been reading in literature.

The importance of daily classes ∞

All dancers – not only students, but even the most famous stars of the greatest ballet companies in the world – take a class every day. Professional dancers have to keep their bodies lithe and strong all the time, even when they are not performing for several weeks or are on holiday, otherwise they will stiffen up. This means they risk injury once they start to dance again. Dancers need a lot of self-discipline to keep themselves in shape. Working dancers usually take class for an hour and a half every day, under the eye of another experienced senior member of the company. Student dancers usually have even longer daily classes, because they have so much to learn.

It is very important to start limbering up before class begins. Then, at the *barre*, all dancers work through every joint, muscle and bone to make their bodies move smoothly and safely. Always keeping in time to the music, they start with *pliés*, working their feet, ankles, knees and hips, then progressing up through their spine, neck, shoulders and arms. As they warm up, their joints become looser, so they can stretch further, move faster and jump higher.

The teachers are constantly correcting the dancers' movements, helping them to aim for perfection. As the class continues, the dancers' balance gradually improves and they can retain more difficult poses without the support of the *barre*.

Building strength & skill

A dancer must be as precise as a scientist. She must be able to hold a difficult pose without even one finger out of place. She must not only move elegantly but, for example in *battements serrés*, be able to strike the correct points of her ankles with her toes – the front, the back, the front, the back – very quickly and accurately, almost like the flickering of a butterfly's wings.

Later on, she will need to make the same *ballon* movements mid-air in the middle of a jump. 'Your brains must reach down to your toes,' the teacher says.

The need for precision and absolutely correct style is one of the most important aspects of learning about classical ballet. This is why it is vital to have a good teacher.

In order to perform all the magnificent leaps and turns of classical ballet, pupils will first have to work hard to perfect the basic movements.

A wise Russian teacher at the school points out that there are no short cuts. Pupils must study with absolute devotion at this early age to succeed. If they are lazy about detail now, they will be very disappointed when they get older and find that there are advanced steps or leaps they will never achieve.

Higher & faster ∽

Now the dancers are truly warmed up and their joints are looser still. It is time for *grands battements*: the swinging of one leg high to the front, back to the ground, then to the side and behind, and to the side again.

This movement is easiest when the music is fast; to lift the legs very slowly into the correct position is more difficult. The dancers listen carefully to the music to know just how much longer they will have to make the movement last. They must count the beats of the music and everyone's legs must arrive together at the highest point on the correct note.

While the dancers on one side of the room are under the eagle eye of the teacher, those waiting for their turn continue to exercise and improve their stretches. A professional dancer is always working, even when the teacher is looking elsewhere. (Some people even practise pointing their toes under their desks during lessons or when reading a book or watching television.)

Turn-out ❦

The secret of many difficult and advanced movements in classical ballet is the dancers' turn-out at the hips. These boys are practising a special stretching exercise to expand their hip joints so they can achieve even more impressive positions.

Turn-out at the hips is one of the natural gifts of true ballet dancers. Most people are born with less flexible joints and will never be able to swivel hips and knees outward. Nothing must be forced, otherwise crippling back problems can result. However, regular hard work will improve suppleness.

Many of the most beautiful positions in classical dance require good turn-out, as well as balance, as demonstrated here by ballerina Darcey Bussell, who was a pupil at the Royal Ballet School not so very long ago.

The splits ∞

When the work at the *barre* is finished, the dancers like to give themselves a really good stretch before the second part of the class.

By the time the students have been at the school for several months, almost all the children can achieve the splits. However, with daily practice, they should all soon succeed.

There are many other kinds of stretches. It takes real strength, as well as a lot of practice, for this fifteen-year-old boy to hold his leg

high in exactly the correct position while his teacher explains (for two long minutes) precisely which tiny muscles need strengthening and how he can improve his stretch even further.

Though it is rare to see the splits on the floor of the stage, this stretch is a crucial part of dance – and can be seen in, for example, a *grand jeté* or an extension.

Port de bras
& arabesque

In every ballet class, dancers practise *port de bras*, which means the way the arms are lifted and moved in coordination with the rest of the body and the head. The arms of dancers are just as important as feet. 'You must follow your hand with your eyes,' the teacher says. 'Imagine you have a balloon under your arms, soft and strong.'

All the time, whatever difficult exercises they're doing with their feet or legs, the dancers have to maintain graceful arm positions. 'Your elbows must disappear. Your arms should look as if they have no bones,' they are told.

Arms in *arabesque* must be part of the flowing curve from toes through to the fingers. This first-year boy has just landed from a travelling jump into an *arabesque en fondu* – even at speed he must place his arms correctly.

Jumps

The jumps begin with the vertical *temps levés* – not as simple as they look. Toes and insteps must be stretched, the legs turned out, arms in place, and the head and back correctly held.

The secret of any jump, vertical or travelling, is to start with a *plié*. In a fast sequence of movements, you would use only a shallow *plié*, but for a higher vertical jump it is a different matter.

'Think of the floor as a friend who is going to almost push you into the air,' the teacher says. 'A good strong *plié* is like a long fuse for a rocket – the deeper you bend the higher you jump.'

Gradually the pupils learn many different and exciting jumps. None of them is more thrilling than the high-speed *grand jeté*.

Both boys and girls are told to leap high and land as light as air. In a sequence of leaps across the stage, a dancer should touch down silently, like the soft landing of a balloon which then floats off again. Lightness in take-off and landing (known as *ballon*) is part of the secret of classical dance and takes years to master fully. True *ballon* is achieved only by great dancers. The teachers try to help their pupils understand what *ballon* feels like: 'That was correct but it didn't flow. How do you make writing flow? You join it up. The end of a jump is the beginning of the next one.'

Starting on pointe

The hard toe of the *pointe* shoe is made from layers of canvas and glue which form a 'block'. The shoes are finished in satin, which wears through quickly. (A ballerina dancing in *Swan Lake* may go through three pairs of shoes in just one performance.) *Pointe* shoes are expensive, so young dancers darn the tips of theirs to make them last longer.

The youngest girls know that it is dangerous to use *pointe* shoes until their feet are ready. For the first few weeks of term, they have worked very hard at strengthening and stretching their feet. Their ankles too must develop more holding power.

After long preparation all their hard work pays off and at last their feet are strong enough. Their teacher checks that each shoe fits perfectly, that they have sewn the ribbon in the correct place and that the shoes are tied with not a single end or 'ear' showing.

The first week, they stay on *pointe* for only about fifteen minutes. They bend into *pliés*, then spring up on their toes. The first exercises are at the *barre*, then they move into the centre.

It will take a lot of practice to stand up straight on *pointe*, to keep their feet perfectly vertical with no 'sickling' to the sides, to keep their arms in position and to walk elegantly in time to the music. It will be many weeks before they can move easily and correctly, and months before they are really dancing.

In their second year they will be able to dance quite advanced steps on *pointe*. And by the time they are fifteen or sixteen, they will be working in *pointe* shoes more than in soft ones. Gradually they will start to try to hold poses like the stars of the Royal Ballet.

Dancing on *pointe* allows the girls to give an impression of ethereal lightness and delicacy. They are told, 'Even though your shoes have clumpy blocks on the ends, you've got to dance exquisitely, as if you are on needles.'

Pirouettes

Turning round and round at high speed on one leg is one of the most exciting ballet movements, both for audiences to watch and for dancers to perform. Boys pirouette on *demi-pointe*. Girls, once they have mastered balance and perfect positions, pirouette on full *pointe*. The pointed toes of the 'working' leg neatly touch the knee of the supporting leg, which must be perfectly vertical. The skill is to be able to keep turning without getting giddy, creating one circle after another without pausing.

To pirouette, the dancer sinks into a *demi-plié*, starts to turn her shoulders and body, then whizzes her head in a half-circle so that its weight pulls the rest of her body round. As she spins she quickly anchors her eyes on some mark on the wall or scenery ahead of her.

This 'spotting' helps the dancers to keep a sense of where they are on the stage and also to count the number of turns they have done. They must, of course, finish in perfect, elegant control, ready for turns in the opposite direction or for the next *enchaînement* of steps.

Advanced dancers learn more complicated turns, such as the *fouetté*, in which they whip their leg out at right angles, then back to the knee, again and again as they turn. In some ballets, such as *Swan Lake*, a dancer will have to spin round in more than thirty *fouettés* non-stop, at high speed, all in the same direction. *Tours en l'air*, almost always performed by men, involve leaping up vertically and turning in a perfect position high above the stage before landing elegantly and lightly to perform more brilliant and complicated steps.

Pas de deux

When they are about fifteen years old, the boys and girls start to learn the techniques of dancing as partners.

The male dancer is best known for his athletic leaps and exciting speed on stage. Another important role is skilfully partnering the ballerina while she performs her most daring and beautiful poses and balances.

First, the boy has to learn how to support the girl delicately but firmly. He must appear to hold her only lightly, yet she must be perfectly secure. This is called 'supported *adage*' and is a training for most of the romantic partnerships in the great classical ballets: for instance, when Cinderella is falling in love or the Sugar Plum Fairy is dancing with her prince in *The Nutcracker*.

Learning to lift 🙰

Learning to lift the girls is the next skill for the boys to master. At first they often work with two boys and a girl rather than in pairs.

They are taught to strengthen their upper bodies in a scientific manner so that they develop their power without spoiling the sleek form needed for classical dance. Male dancers must not develop hefty shoulder muscles like a wrestler, yet they must be strong enough to lift the girls high above their head.

In traditional ballets like *The Sleeping Beauty* there are always some wonderful and exciting lifts. In new ballets, even more daring feats are required. Though the shapes they make are original, they are dangerous and sometimes even impossible for dancers who have not had a full *pas de deux* training. Only the senior students of the Upper School attempt these difficult high lifts.

On stage, of course, the Royal Ballet dancers make everything look easy, but it is risky unless everyone is very well prepared. Even professional dancers sometimes get injured while performing. Ballet is like sport: it is exciting, but it needs good nerves and absolute precision.

Choreography ∞ making new ballets

The person who creates a new ballet is called a choreographer. A ballet can be a long story performed in three acts, like *Swan Lake*, or very short (from just a few minutes to half an hour or so, often depending on the length of the music selected).

Royal Ballet School pupils all learn choreography. Many of them want to create their own short ballets. For choreography competitions each pupil finds a piece of music and listens to it over and over again until they know every note. Then they start to invent stories and dance ideas.

At first all the young choreographers work on their own with their chosen dancers. Then they have workshops where the teachers help them get their dancers to make the most of the ideas.

The best ballets are selected for the annual choreography competition. Costumes are provided from the wardrobe room, which has a huge collection from past productions. The brilliant wardrobe mistress can run up about twenty new costumes in a week if necessary. She enjoys helping the young choreographers to realize their ideas.

Final rehearsals are on the stage. The teachers give advice until the last moment, making sure the standard is professional.

All the ballets are good enough to win prizes and it is a very hard job for the judges to decide. Everyone, winner or loser, is encouraged to continue with another ballet soon. It is very important that the pupils get lots of opportunities, because they will be the choreographers as well as the dancers of the future.

Other dance styles ∞

The pupils also learn many other dance styles so that they can perform anything required by the variety of choreographers they will work with during their dancing careers.

The study of contemporary dance is especially important. Many of today's dancers and choreographers prefer the more spontaneous, looser styles of contemporary dance to the strict discipline of ballet. They create all sorts of new, interesting and challenging shapes in their dancing, rarely wearing *pointe* shoes and often performing in bare feet.

Not all pupils of the school will be able to get into the Royal Ballet Company; some might not even get into a ballet company at all. Inevitably, a few dance pupils grow into the wrong shape – perhaps their legs will become too sturdy, or their shoulders too broad for the elegance of classical dance. They may, however, use their ballet training and their musical studies to have a successful career in contemporary dance companies or in musicals or cabaret.

One thing is certain, though: while a classically trained dancer can adapt with special brilliance to all sorts of contemporary, jazz and tap dancing, it does not work the other way round. For classical dancing, long, hard training is the only way.

As well as their daily study of classical dance, ballet dancers need to be familiar with the dances of different countries. In many of the older ballets, the choreography includes folk dances, so it is vital for young dancers to learn different national dance styles, particularly those from Britain, Spain, Hungary and Russia.

These dances are very popular with the public. The pupils of the Royal Ballet School give performances every summer and raise money for charity.

Dancing for television ∞ Peter and the Wolf

Choreographer Matthew Hart, an ex-pupil of the Royal Ballet School, has invented several ballets for the pupils. His *Peter and the Wolf* (to the exciting music of the Russian composer Sergei Prokofiev) is to be filmed for television at the school.

First, the children have to learn their parts and this takes several weeks. Mr Hart, a superb dancer himself, teaches every step to the cast. Then, after weeks of rehearsal, the television crews arrive with huge cameras and a vast array of lights.

Two of the dance studios have been converted into a television studio, with projected backgrounds of forests and trees. For weeks, the human Trees have been rehearsing holding just sticks in their hands. Now their arms become like real branches and they are transformed by television make-up artists, who have been given designs of how the faces should be painted on to the dancers.

The story is about a mischievous boy called Peter who lives on the edge of the forest with his grandfather. The lovely, dancing emerald-green Meadows want Peter to come and play, but his grandfather orders Peter to stay at home, to keep him away from the fierce Wolf. Naughty Peter slips away, joined by his friend Little Bird, who always manages to escape a stalking black Cat. The Wolf suddenly appears from among the Trees of the forest. A stupid and vain little Duck jumps out of her pond in fright. The Wolf catches the Duck and swallows her in one gulp. Some passing hunters help Peter and his friends to make a trap with a rope. They catch the Wolf and march him off to the zoo.

Dancing for television seems much less exciting after many hours of filming. One of the Trees says, 'I'd prefer double science every day to all this waiting around.'

The choreographer starts to worry that if the television producer makes them do any more repeats the children will 'lose their sparkle and fizz'. But the ballet teachers gently encourage everyone: 'This is professional work and you have to keep going like proper professionals until we get it absolutely right.'

It will be a whole year before the young dancers see the results of their hard work on the television.

Anastasia ∞

Sometimes pupils from the school are chosen to take part in professional productions with the Royal Opera Ballet Company in London.

Anastasia, a modern ballet by Sir Kenneth MacMillan, calls for acting as well as dancing. It tells the story of the Russian princess Anastasia and her little brother, the Tsarevich. In 1918, during the Russian Revolution, the Russian royal family were assassinated by the Bolsheviks, but some people think that Anastasia survived.

Part of the ballet is about Anastasia's early life, when she is with her family on the royal yacht. The young prince is rather sickly and everyone fusses over him a great deal.

In deciding who is to dance the Tsarevich, various factors have been taken into account. Some old photographs exist of the real prince; as well as being a good actor and an excellent dancer, the boy must look something like the Tsarevich.

Two younger boys are learning the prince's part at the same time. They will take turns performing at the Royal Opera House. Each of them will be partnered by a different ballerina in the part of Anastasia.

The boys both get a run-through on stage as the prince, but not a full dress rehearsal. They have to get used to the sailor's hat and floppy trousers in the studio, then wear them on stage for the first time in a real performance. It is tricky to keep the sailor's hat in place while performing.

The last act of the ballet shows Anastasia after her escape, when she is a refugee, poor and almost mad. The audience see her having terrifying nightmares about the past (acted by the dancers). At one point the little prince is hurled across the stage high into the air, to be caught by a dreaded figure from Anastasia's childhood, the evil priest Rasputin.

Swan Lake ∾

Most years, a group of the younger girls join the *corps de ballet* as Little Swans in *Swan Lake*. It is very exciting to be chosen, and no one minds that they have to give up their free time until they know their parts perfectly. Costumes are brought from the theatre and fitted at the school.

They work and work, week after week. Their teacher reminds them that they must not make a single mistake on stage. This is not only because of the audience, but also because they are going to be performing with one of the greatest ballet companies in the world.

At last it is time to start work with the grown-up Swans in the Royal Ballet rehearsal studio. They peel off their tracksuits and shiver with nerves before they are called.

The Swan Princess, ballerina Deborah Bull, is very friendly. She was at the Royal Ballet School herself and can imagine exactly how the little ones feel.

A week later, rehearsals begin on the vast stage of the Royal Opera House. The girls share a dressing room full of mirrors, and learn to pin on their own headdresses.

They must always remember to check that their shoe ribbons are safe, and give them an extra stitch before going on stage. Anyone who trips will spoil the ballet for the audience; they also might get seriously injured, and even cause another dancer to fall.

Again, there is no full dress rehearsal, but several semi-costume stage rehearsals with different ballerinas in the lead each day. The Little Swans wear their costumes and headdresses so that they are used to dancing in them before the

performances. Dancers need to keep their muscles and joints warm and there is a lot of waiting around in rehearsals, so although the Swan Princess is rehearsing in costume she keeps on her leg warmers. One of the Swans in the *corps de ballet*, frightened of draughts, is wearing her jacket!

The Little Swans are inspired as they dance for the first time with a live orchestra. It is certainly very different from the piano in the rehearsal studios.

This is just a glimpse of the performer's life, but it is what everyone is working towards. Being chosen for a part means missing all sorts of treats, because the young dancers will be in the dance studio getting every finger, every smile, the direction of their eyes, the tilt of their head, the height of their jump, everything as near perfect as humanly possible. They will have to put up with long journeys in a minibus to the theatre, warming up in different places, waiting about, doing classes backstage. But in return they will experience the thrill of performing for an audience with truly great dancers all around them.

Summer performances

During the last weeks of the summer term all pupils work on ballets for a range of public performances, both at the Royal Opera House and elsewhere. Every year a well-known choreographer creates a new ballet for the school.

The Spider's Feast by David Bintley uses children of different ages together. They take the parts of insects, the youngest boys as ants and the girls as mayflies.

The fourteen-year-olds perform Tweedle-Dum, Tweedle-Dee and Alice in Sir Frederick Ashton's hilarious choreography of *Alice in Wonderland*.

The graduates at the top of the school often perform dances from great classical ballets like *Giselle* or *Checkmate*, which was choreographed by Dame Ninette de Valois, the founder of the Royal Ballet School and the Royal Ballet Company.

End of term

Ballet practice has to continue during the holidays. Everyone is told to keep flexible and supple. They must work for a little while every day wherever they are, even if they live in a small flat or are travelling abroad.

When they are sixteen, the best pupils will move up to the Upper School. Most of the pupils of the Upper School, after two further years of extremely hard training, will go to different dance companies all over the world. Some will become professional choreographers. Some of the Upper School pupils will have chosen the course for ballet teachers; many Royal Ballet School teaching graduates run their own ballet schools in Britain and abroad.

Only the very best Royal Ballet School students will be invited to join the Royal Ballet Company. Even then they will go on studying new roles, learning more and more difficult techniques. Great dancers are never satisfied. They will always want to leap higher, to try daring new lifts or to achieve even more brilliant footwork.

The eighteen-year-olds who are selected for the Royal Ballet Company have studied the choreography for many famous ballets, but will find they are still almost beginners beside the more senior dancers. However, gradually they will learn more and more different parts in many different ballets, old and new.

These young dancers will carry on the great Royal Ballet traditions, learned at the school and in the company, and passed on from generation to generation.

Dance over the centuries

Dance is an international language that everyone can understand, because ideas are communicated and stories told through movement rather than words. Children all over the world can learn the same steps and understand each other through dance, wherever they come from.

The beauty of dance has delighted human beings since the very beginnings of time. Dancing is depicted in cave paintings tens of thousands of years old and in carvings on the ancient temples of countries as diverse as Egypt, India, Greece and Cambodia. In this early Indian stone carving, the dancer is just as turned-out at the hips as the pupils of the Royal Ballet School.

People have always marked important occasions with dance: in spring they would dance to celebrate the planting of the crops; in autumn, at harvest time, to celebrate the gathering of corn for bread and grapes for wine. In European royal courts, graceful courtiers used to minuet elegantly to please their princes.

The true art of ballet began to develop in Italy about five hundred years ago out of these courtiers' dances. By the seventeenth century, ballet was popular in France and by the beginning of the nineteenth century some French ballerinas had started dancing on their toes. Later in the nineteenth century, the Russians created magical ballets such as *Swan Lake*, *The Sleeping Beauty* and *The Nutcracker*, the much-loved classics which are still performed today.

Early in the twentieth century the touring Diaghilev company thrilled the Western world with all sorts of exciting new ballet ideas. Sergei Diaghilev inspired Ninette de Valois, who founded Sadler's Wells, then the Royal Ballet School and company. He also inspired the great choreographer George Balanchine, who started the School of American Ballet and New York City Ballet. Now there are classical companies all over Europe, in North and South America, Australia, New Zealand and many countries of Asia and Africa too.

Glossary ∞

Because ballet was developed in France, French remains the language used to describe almost all the ballet steps, jumps and turns.

Arabesque A pose in which the dancer stands on one leg with the other raised behind. The arms are in graceful, complementary positions. There are several forms of *arabesque*.

Ballon Bounciness and lightness which make a good dancer seem almost airborne.

Battement Beating movements of the leg which may be a fast, fluttering action (*battement serré*) or slow, with a high lift, with the bent or straight knee of the working leg.

Corps de ballet The large group of dancers who act as a 'chorus' in the ballet, dancing usually as a group. Most dancers begin their career in the corps before going on to dance solo parts.

Demi-pointe Balancing on the ball of the foot.

Enchaînement A series of steps, turns and/or jumps linked together.

Extension Lifting the working leg to front, side or back, demonstrating flexibility in various positions. Only a very advanced dancer (like ballerina Darcey Bussell) can achieve a fully vertical extension by lifting one leg behind her. (The illustration on page 27 shows this step, called an *arabesque penchée*.)

Fondu A slow *plié* on the supporting leg. *Fondu* means 'melted'.

Fouetté A brilliant turning movement where the dancer is on one leg and the other (pointed) foot whips in and out from the knee to help the body turn.

Jeté Meaning thrown, this word is used to describe different movements such as the *grand jeté*, a travelling leap across the floor with one leg thrown ahead of the other.

On pointe Dancing on the tips of the toes.

Pas de deux A sequence for two dancers.

Pirouette A turn on one foot.

Plié A position where the knees are bent over the toes. *Pliés* are essential to warm the muscles and are practised at the beginning of every dance class. They are also used to give enough spring to leap high.

Port de bras Translates literally as carriage of the arms. *Port de bras* exercises involve correct arm, hand and finger movements in relation to the position of head and body.

Révérences The formal bow or curtsy made to the teacher, the pianist and the audience at the end of a class or performance.

Temps levés A hop or spring on the spot.

Tour en l'air A turn in the air. This movement is mainly performed by male dancers.

Working leg The supporting leg takes the weight of the body, while the working leg performs the dance movement.

Acknowledgements

Camilla Jessel wishes to thank Dame Merle Parke and all the staff at the Royal Ballet School
for their generous help in making this book possible. She thanks the many children in the
photographs and regrets there was not room in these pages for everyone in the school to appear.
She is grateful too to the dancers of the Royal Ballet and their helpful Press Office.
Special thanks are due to Christine Beckley, Richard Glassman, Shirley Graham and Patricia Linton.

The publisher would like to thank the Bridgeman Art Library, London,
for their kind permission to reproduce the Carving of Dancing Goddess (stone) Soninathpur,
Karnataka, India/Bridgeman Art Library, London/Dinodia Picture Agency, Bombay.

For details of auditions please write to:
The Auditions Department
The Royal Ballet School
155 Talgarth Road
Baron's Court
London W14 9DE
United Kingdom

Auditions are held for the following age groups:
a) The Royal Ballet School – Lower School (at ten years for eleven-year-old entry)
b) The Royal Ballet School – Upper School (at fifteen years for sixteen-year-old entry)
c) The Royal Ballet Junior Associates (eight years old and upwards)
d) The Royal Ballet Junior Summer School (nine years old)
e) The Royal Ballet Senior Associates and/or Senior Summer School (fourteen years old)